W9-AGM-086

SHORT TALES
Fables

The Lion and the Mouse

Adapted by Shannon Eric Denton
Illustrated by Mike Dubisch

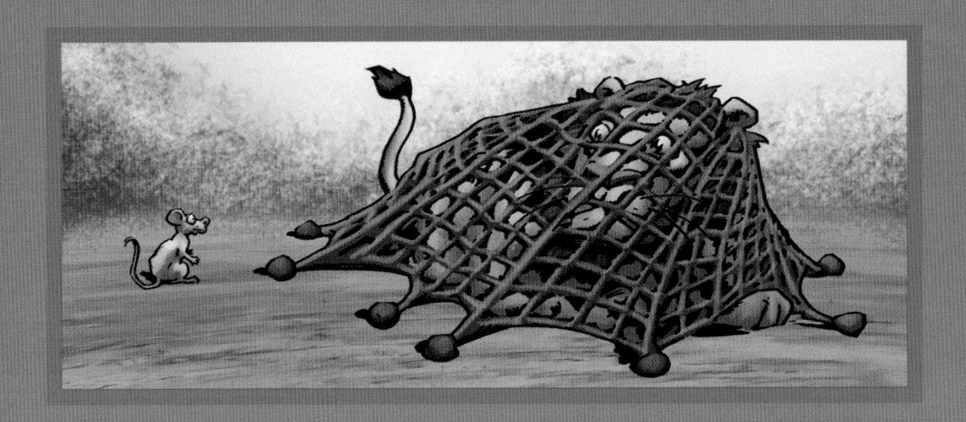

visit us at www.abdopublishing.com

Published by Magic Wagon, a division of the ABDO Group, 8000 West 78th Street, Edina, Minnesota, 55439.

Printed in the United States of America, North Mankato, Minnesota.
092009
012010
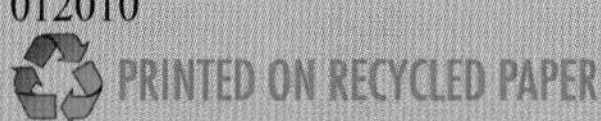

Adapted Text by Shannon Eric Denton
Illustrations by Mike Dubisch
Colors by Wes Hartman
Edited by Stephanie Hedlund
Interior Layout by Kristen Fitzner Denton
Book Design and Packaging by Shannon Eric Denton

Library of Congress Cataloging-in-Publication Data

Denton, Shannon Eric.
The lion and the mouse / adapted by Shannon Eric Denton ; illustrated by Mike Dubisch.
p. cm. -- (Short tales. Fables)
ISBN 978-1-60270-554-8
[1. Fables. 2. Folklore.] I. Dubisch, Michael, ill. II. Aesop. III. Title.
PZ8.2.D34Li 2010
398.2--dc22
[E]

2008032318

One day, a bored mouse was watching a sleeping lion.

The mouse decided it would be fun to surf down the lion.

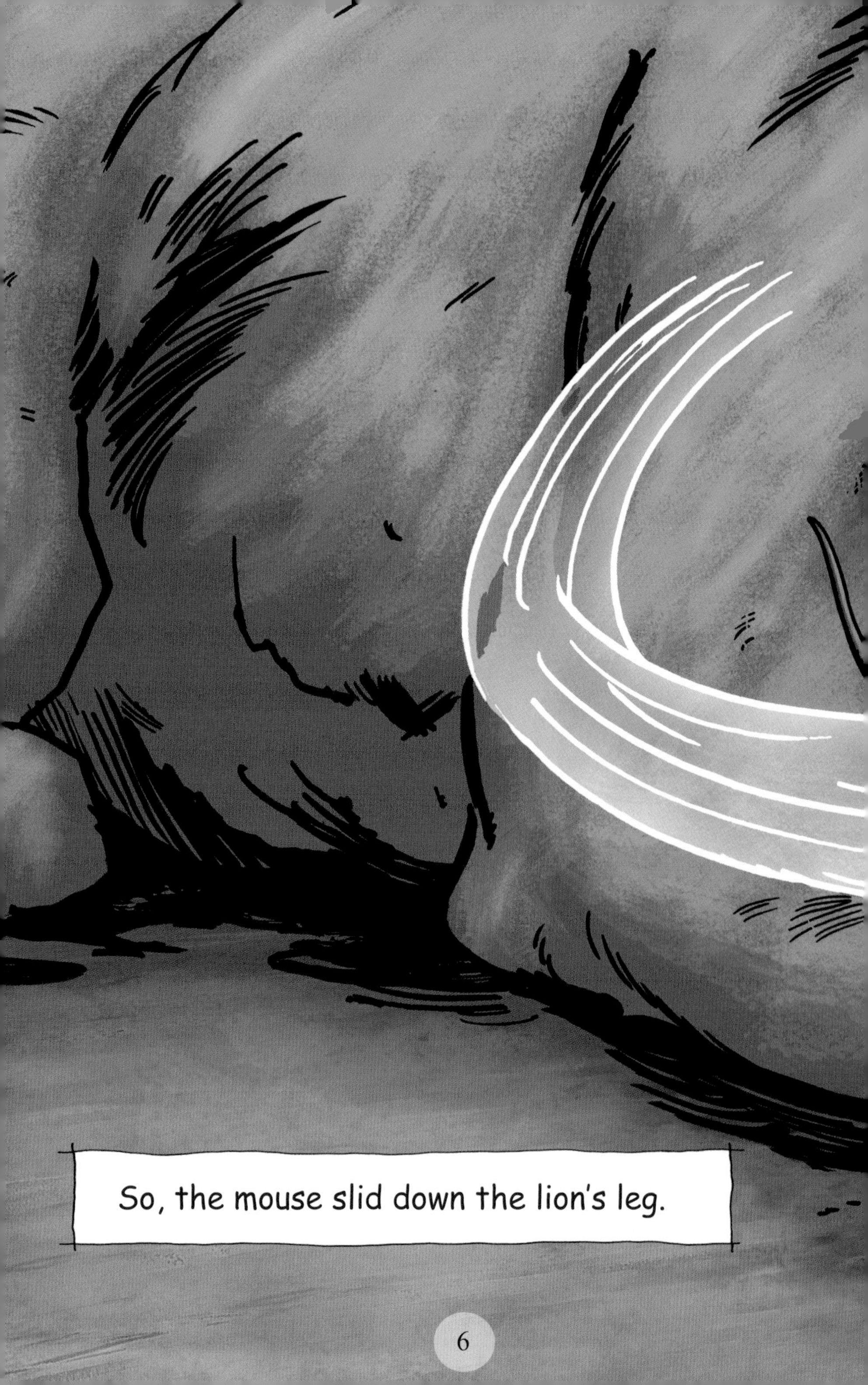
So, the mouse slid down the lion's leg.

Suddenly, the lion woke up
and saw the mouse.

The lion caught the mouse with his paw.

"Please, please let me go!" the mouse begged.

"I'll do anything to pay you back!" the mouse cried.

The lion found the mouse's begging funny.

"Okay, you may go," the lion said.

That afternoon, the lion continued on his way.

He was soon trapped in a hunter's net.

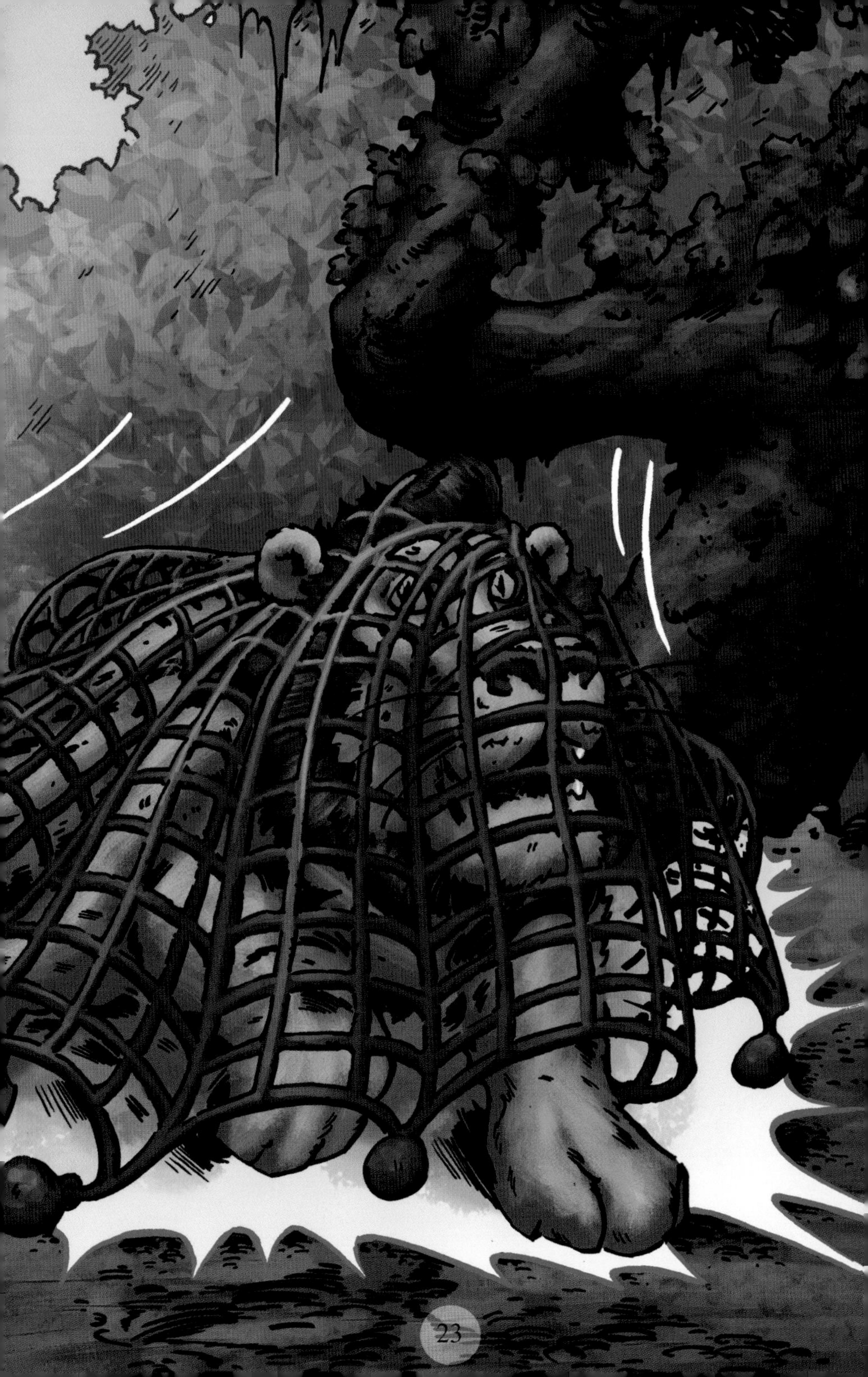

The lion roared his anger,
and the mouse heard him.

The mouse chewed through the ropes and freed the lion.

The lion was surprised the
mouse had freed him.

Together, the lion and his new friend walked away.

The moral of the story is:

Little friends may prove to be great friends.